Nightmare Nurse!

Corey doesn't understand why his dad warns, "Don't ever get sick at Granny's." Since Corey was dropped off at her house for the weekend, Granny Marsha has seemed like a such a nice lady. She bakes cookies, makes Corey's favorite dinner. Yup. Looks like it's going to be a great weekend.

Until Corey starts to sneeze and sniffle. And Granny starts looking at him in a creepy way, saying she knows how to *take care* of sick children.

Will Corey recover? Or will Granny scare the germs out of him permanently?

Grab a tissue and read on to find out!

Also from R. L. Stine

The Beast
The Beast 2

Available from MINSTREL Books

R·L·STINE'S
GHOSTS OF FEAR STREET®

DON'T EVER GET SICK AT GRANNY'S

A Parachute Press Book

A
MINSTREL®
BOOK

Published by POCKET BOOKS
New York   London   Toronto   Sydney   Tokyo   Singapore

A MINSTREL PAPERBACK *Original*

 A Minstrel Paperback published by
POCKET BOOKS, a division of Simon & Schuster Inc.
1230 Avenue of the Americas, New York, NY 10020

Copyright © 1997 by Parachute Press, Inc.

DON'T EVER GET SICK AT GRANNY'S WRITTEN BY
JAHNNA N. MALCOLM

All rights reserved, including the right to reproduce
this book or portions thereof in any form whatsoever.
For information address Pocket Books, 1230 Avenue
of the Americas, New York, NY 10020

ISBN: 0-671-00188-4

First Minstrel Books paperback printing January 1997

10 9 8 7 6 5 4 3 2 1

FEAR STREET is a registered trademark of
Parachute Press, Inc.

A MINSTREL BOOK and colophon are registered trademarks
of Simon & Schuster Inc.

Cover art by Mark Garro

Printed in the U.S.A.

R·L·STINE'S

GHOSTS OF FEAR STREET®

DON'T EVER GET
SICK AT GRANNY'S

I

"**C**orey! Quit kicking the back of my seat!" Dad ordered from the front of the car.

"And get your elbow off *my* side," my sister Meg whined.

"And roll up that window," Mom added. "It's blowing my hair all over the place."

"Why is everybody yelling at me?" I wailed. "I'm not doing anything!"

I scrunched my body into a tight ball and stared out the window. I didn't want to come on this trip. I wanted to stay home in Shadyside with my friends.

But no! Meg had to audition for stupid ballet school. So we all had to cram into our stupid car and drive halfway across the stupid state of Pennsylvania in ninety-degree heat. With no air-conditioning. *That* broke the second we left Fear Street.

"I'm hot!" I grumbled after we'd driven about five more miles. "When are we going to get there?"

"You know how long it takes to get to Granny Marsha's." Mom turned around in the front seat to face me. "It's exactly four hours from our front door to hers."

I stared at her. "Granny Marsha," I repeated.

Mom nodded.

I stared at her some more. *Granny Marsha?* I had no idea who Mom was talking about. My brain was a total blank.

"Granny Marsha is going to be happy to see you," Mom gushed, ruffling my blond hair with her hand.

I hate it when Mom does that. I'm twelve years old, but she treats me like I'm four.

I ducked my head away from her hand. "When was the last time I saw Granny?"

Mom gazed at me in disbelief. "Don't tell me you don't remember!"

"Okay, I won't," I joked. But I really *didn't* remember.

Meg rolled her eyes. "Cor-ey. We went to Granny Marsha's house last July for your birthday. She gave you a ton of presents."

I faked a smile and nodded. "Oh, right . . ."

This was getting weird. How could I forget my own grandmother?

Meg opened a carton of nonfat yogurt and dipped her spoon into it. "Granny always gives you great gifts. Skateboards, basketballs, that dartboard. She only sends me checks."

"Granny gave me my skateboard?" I gasped. Why couldn't I remember that? I had practically lived on that skateboard for an entire year.

"Granny Marsha sure is something," Dad said, chuckling. "Right, Corey?"

"Heh-heh. Yeah, she sure is!" She's something, all right. A total stranger! I swallowed hard. I couldn't believe this! I had absolutely no idea who my Granny Marsha was.

Mom slapped at my knee. "Come on, Corey. Stop kidding us."

"Uh, right." I sat straight up in my seat. "I'm just kidding."

How could I tell my family I couldn't remember my own grandmother? They'd think I was nuts. I glanced sideways at Meg. She was staring at me suspiciously.

"It's a joke!" I insisted, a little too loudly. "Okay? A joke!"

Meg winced. "You don't have to shout." She

tapped Mom on the shoulder. "Mom! Tell Corey not to yell at me!"

I rolled down my window. Maybe some fresh air would make my brain kick into action. Maybe then I'd remember.

"Corey?" Mom warned, pointing at the window.

"Oh, right. Your hair." I rolled the window back up.

The car felt like an oven. Every part of me was sweating. I shoved my face over the front seat. "Mom, feel my forehead. Maybe I've got a fever."

"Don't even joke about being sick," Dad said. He gave me a stern look in the rearview mirror.

"I'm not joking!" I moaned, slumping back in the seat. "I'm hot."

Dad and Mom exchanged worried glances. "You've probably just been in the car too long," Mom suggested.

"I'm sure that's it," Dad agreed. He hit the turn signal. We pulled off the Pennsylvania turnpike onto a bumpy side road.

The plan was to drop me at Granny Marsha's house in the country. Then Mom and Dad would drive Meg on to Philadelphia for her tryout for the Pennsylvania State Ballet School. They were going to stay at a hotel. With a pool.

"Why can't I stay at the hotel with you guys?" I

4

whined. "Why do I have to go to Granny Marsha's?"

"Now, we've gone over this a hundred times," Mom said. "This is a very big event for Meg. If she is accepted at this school, it's almost certain she'll be accepted to the Pennsylvania Ballet Company. We can't have you moping around the dance studio. You'll ruin Meg's concentration."

"Meg can't have any distractions," Dad added.

I glanced at my sister. Meg sat with her chin tilted up and her auburn hair pulled into a tight knot on top of her head.

I made a pig face at her.

Meg stuck her tongue out at me.

"Look, I don't want to go to those stupid auditions," I argued. "I'll just hang out at the hotel."

"Now, Corey." Mom sighed. "You know that's not possible."

I slumped back in my seat. It wasn't fair. Why couldn't I go to the hotel with my family?

Dad was watching me in the rearview mirror. "Hey, Corey, don't take it so hard," he said sympathetically. "You love Granny Marsha. You two are going to have a great time."

He flicked on the turn signal again and pulled the car into a gravel driveway.

"Look, Corey," Mom declared. "We're here."

The car turned toward a gray house with white trim and a bright red door. A narrow green lawn stretched the length of the driveway. I craned my neck hoping to get a glimpse of Granny. Maybe if I saw her in person, I'd remember her.

Mom flipped down the visor mirror and quickly ran a brush through her windblown hair. As she brushed, she gave me her standard last-minute instructions. "Now, I expect you to be polite, keep your feet off the furniture, and pick up after yourself. Granny Marsha will appreciate that."

"Just be careful of one thing," Dad warned as he put the car in park.

I leaned forward. "What one thing?"

Mom and Dad slowly turned and gazed at me. Their expressions made my heart skip a beat. For a second I didn't even recognize them. Their faces were frozen in strange masks of fear.

Mom nodded her head slowly up and down as Dad narrowed his eyes in deep concentration. His voice dropped to a hoarse whisper.

"Don't ever get sick at Granny's."

2

"**D**-d-d-dad?" I stammered. "What do you mean, I shouldn't get sick?"

But Dad didn't hear me. He and Mom both turned back around in their seats. Dad furiously honked the horn to call Granny Marsha.

The front door swung open. A plump woman wearing overalls, and a gardening hat and gloves, burst out of the house. She looked like your average sixty-year-old grandmother, except for her red high-top sneakers.

"Welcome!" Granny cried, waving a gloved hand at us. "You made it."

I've never seen that woman before in my life, I thought, squinting at the gray-haired lady. She jogged toward the car. The closer she got the more certain I was that we had never, ever met.

"Granny!" Dad and Mom were out of the car in a heartbeat. Meg was right behind them. All of them hugged and kissed Granny Marsha, whose cheeks flushed pink with pleasure.

"You must be parched!" Granny exclaimed, once everyone finished hugging everyone else. "Come inside. I've got an ice-cold pitcher of lemonade."

I slumped down in the backseat. I figured if I didn't get out of the car, maybe they'd forget about me. Then I'd get to go with them to the hotel after all.

No such luck.

"Corey! What are you doing in there?" Meg scolded, flinging open my car door. "Come out and say hello to Granny Marsha."

"I don't want to," I replied.

Meg put her hands on her hips. "And why not?"

"Because I'd rather sit in this car and sweat." I folded my arms across my chest and glared at Meg. I could just picture her swimming in the hotel pool and ordering sodas from room service.

"I've got an idea," I announced, raising one finger. "Why don't you stay here with Granny, and I'll go swimming at the hotel?"

Meg glanced over her shoulder to see if Granny

had heard me. "Get out right now," she snapped at me, "or you'll hurt Granny Marsha's feelings."

Mom suddenly appeared behind Meg. "Corey! There you are! Come out and give Granny Marsha a big kiss."

If there's one thing I hate, it's kissing people. Major gross-out! I bolted out of the car, but Granny caught hold of me.

"Corey, don't worry about kissing," she said. "We can stick to high fives." She stuck out her hand and I high-fived her.

Hmmmm. Maybe Granny Marsha wasn't so bad after all.

We followed Granny into the house. We were all going to have lunch, and then my family would continue on to Philadelphia. Without me.

"Corey, I made your favorite food." Granny placed a cheeseburger and a huge plate of fries in front of me. "Chow down."

Cheeseburgers! I love cheeseburgers. If all the meals were like this, I guess I could stand hanging out here for a few days.

I took a big messy bite. "Tanks, gwanny," I said with my mouth full. "Dis is delicious."

I practically inhaled my lunch.

"That's what I like to see!" Granny smiled as she gave me seconds of everything. "A good eater."

Mom chuckled. "Corey is definitely that."

Meg, as usual, hardly ate a thing. She kept checking her watch and giving Dad meaningful looks. Finally she stood up. "I don't want to be rude," she announced, "but I think we should leave soon."

Dad nodded and pushed himself back from the table. "Meg's right. It's time we were hitting the trail."

He headed for the door after Meg.

"Wait, Dad!" I leaped up, leaving my half-eaten second burger on my plate. I had to stop him. Something was bugging me, and I had to ask him about it.

Mom stepped in front of me. She handed Granny a piece of paper. "Here's the number of the hotel," she said. "In case of an emergency."

Emergency! Why would there be an emergency?

"I'll just put it here on the fridge," Granny said. She stuck the phone number on the door under a magnet that was shaped like a mouse. She patted me on the back. "But we won't be having any problems here, will we, Corey?"

"Um, no," I mumbled. Dad was already out the front door. I had to catch him. I darted past Mom and out the door.

"Dad!" I called, running into the driveway. "Wait!"

Dad turned and stopped. When I ran up beside him, he clapped me on the back. "We'll see you in a few days, champ."

"Dad," I whispered. I tried to keep my voice down so Granny Marsha wouldn't hear. "What did you mean when you said I shouldn't get sick at—?"

"You be good to Granny Marsha," Mom cut in. She had come up behind me. Now she gave me a big hug and slobbery kiss on the forehead.

I wiped my head with the back of my sleeve. "Dad, listen—"

But Dad was getting into the car. Meg was already in the back seat. I hurried around the car, but Granny was there ahead of me.

"If you want to fill up your gas tank," she said, leaning in his open window, "there's a little Gas 'N' Go two blocks down the road."

"Good idea," Mom said. She blew me another kiss as she got into the car. "We may not have another opportunity before we arrive in Philadelphia."

Seconds later they pulled out of the driveway. And that was it! Whether I liked it or not, I was stuck with Granny for the next two days. She seemed thrilled.

The instant my parents' car disappeared around the corner, Granny clapped her hands together and giggled. "Now that the cat's away, the mice will

11

play. What do you say—do you want to have some fun?"

"Fun?" I shrugged. "Sure. I like fun."

What was I going to say? *No. I want to sit and sulk for two days.*

"Let's refill our glasses, and then I'll show you my entertainment center," she suggested, walking back to the house. "It's pretty impressive, if I do say so myself."

Boy, she wasn't kidding. Granny led me into her den, which had a big-screen TV, two VCRs, and a state-of-the-art surround-sound system.

"Whoa!" I let out a low whistle. Okay, I was impressed. And surprised. Who would think a grandma would have so much cool equipment?

I sipped my lemonade and checked out her living room. It looked pretty comfortable. Two over-stuffed chairs with foot rests faced the TV screen.

Granny Marsha picked up a plate of cookie crumbs from the coffee table. "When I'm not out gardening or walking, I become a regular couch potato."

My kind of person, I thought.

I flipped through the videotapes that were in a floor-to-ceiling tower by the television. She had everything—horror, sci-fi, mysteries—it was great!

"If you want to watch a movie," she said, carrying the plate into the kitchen, "just grab a tape and put it on. I've also got a pool table in the basement and a pinball machine. Later we can make popcorn."

"Popcorn, movies—even pinball. Wow!" I raised my glass to my mouth. Maybe this visit wouldn't be so bad after all.

But just as I was about to take a sip of my drink, something tickled my nose. I sneezed.

Like a shot Granny Marsha reappeared in the doorway.

She narrowed her eyes and took a step toward me. The look in her eyes made my hair stand on end.

"You're not getting sick, are you?" Granny Marsha demanded.

"No!" I insisted. "No way."

Granny stared at me. I shivered. Just a second ago her eyes were a soft blue. Now they resembled cold gray steel. And seemed just as hard.

"Why are you staring at me?" I asked, taking a step backward.

"Are you sick?" Those eyes of hers burned a hole through me. "Tell the truth, Corey. Because if you're sick, I'll have to"—she lowered her voice—*"take care of you."*

"Take care of me?" I repeated.

What did *that* mean?

Being taken care of is usually a good thing. Why did it sound scary when Granny Marsha said it?

I set my lemonade glass down on the coffee table. "Hey, don't worry about me, Granny. I feel just fine. Really."

"I know how to take care of sick little boys," she continued. One corner of her mouth tilted up into a crooked smile. At that moment she looked pretty wacko.

"Sit down," Granny ordered, pointing to the couch.

I dropped into the chair farthest away from Granny. "I'll sit here, thanks."

Granny continued to study me with those cold gray eyes.

I took another sip of my lemonade. And then it happened.

First a tickle.

It started in my nostrils. And traveled quickly upward.

My eyes began to water. I opened them really wide, trying to stop it.

It wasn't working.

My jaw dropped open. My eyes crossed.

I turned my head and squinted with blurry eyes at Granny.

She leaned forward, watching me eagerly.

Now my lip was curling. I couldn't hold it back any longer.

No! Don't do it!

But I couldn't stop myself.

I sneezed!

3

"*A*H-CHOO!*"*

I sneezed so hard my body slammed into the back of the chair. Granny Marsha took a step toward me.

"Sneezes are a warning," Granny said. "Of *bad* things to come."

"I'm okay! Really!" I cried, struggling to my feet. "I have allergies! I'm allergic to your cats."

Granny Marsha squinted those cold gray eyes at me again. "I don't have a cat. You know that."

"Of course," I bluffed. "Then it must be the dust."

"There's no dust in Granny's house," she countered. She raised her hand. Slowly. Very slowly. "Dust wouldn't be good for Granny's patients."

Patients! What patients?

Granny moved closer and closer. Her hand went higher and higher. My eyes grew wide with fright. Suddenly her hand came speeding toward my head. She was going to hit me!

No! I flung my arms up, shielding my face from the blow.

"Corey! You act like I'm going to strike you," Granny scolded. "Would Granny do a thing like that?" She shook her head. "I just want to feel your forehead."

"Oh. Right." I chuckled nervously and lowered my hands. "Go ahead. But I'm totally fine."

She pressed her hand against my forehead. "I don't know—you seem a little warm." She made little clucking noises. "*Too* warm, if you ask me."

I jerked backward. "I'm fine. I'm terrific. I'm just overheated from riding in that hot car. You know," I explained, "the air-conditioning broke down."

Granny folded her arms across her chest. "Just to be safe, I'll keep my eye on you for the rest of the day."

She wasn't kidding.

I spent the afternoon watching videos, and Granny Marsha spent the afternoon watching me. She never left her chair once.

Every time I'd turn to take a sip of my drink, or grab a handful of popcorn, there she was. Staring at me.

"Are you sick yet?" she'd ask with a hopeful smile. It was like she *wanted* me to be sick. She was really giving me the creeps.

Pretty soon I didn't even have to turn around to know she was looking at me. I could feel her eyes drilling holes in the back of my neck.

To make matters worse, that tickling feeling I had in my nose had moved to my throat. And my eyes were getting watery and itchy.

I stared at the TV, but I couldn't really concentrate. Dad's warning kept ringing in my ears.

"Don't ever get sick at Granny's." Why not? What did he mean?

I'm not sick, I told myself. I'm nervous. A strange little old lady in red high-tops is making me a nervous wreck.

I sneaked a look at her out of the corner of my eye. She sat hunched over with her chin stuck out, staring at me. A vulture. That's what she looks like, I thought. One of those cartoon vultures.

"Don't you have stuff you need to do?" I asked.

"It can wait," she replied, narrowing her eyelids to little squinty slits in her face. "*I* can wait. Granny's good at waiting."

I shuddered.

Two hours later Granny called into the living room, "Dinner! It's time to feed that cold," she said, leading me into the kitchen.

"But I don't have a cold," I protested, sitting down at the kitchen table.

"We'll see about that," Granny gushed.

We ate roast chicken and dumplings. Or I did. She barely touched her food, she was so busy watching me.

"I think this is the best chicken I've ever eaten," I said heartily. I wanted to sound really healthy. "I could probably eat a whole chicken by myself."

Granny didn't seem to go for it. She pursed her lips. "Hmmmm," was all she said.

Hmmmm. What did that mean?

Granny continued to stare.

She made me so nervous my hands started to shake. I could barely raise my fork to my mouth.

"You know, you look very pale." Granny leaned across the table with her hand stretched toward my forehead. "*Too* pale."

"I'm always pale," I fibbed, leaning out of her reach. "I'm a very pale person."

Granny Marsha raised an eyebrow.

"I was voted most pale in my class." I held up one hand. "Honest."

She reached out to feel my forehead again, but I thrust my plate into her hands. "Chicken! Chicken makes me pale. And boy, was that good chicken! I bet I ate three helpings at least."

Granny carried our plates to the sink. While she loaded them in the dishwasher, I bolted for the bathroom.

"Can't look pale," I muttered, closing the bathroom door. I hurried to the mirror. "Pale means sick and I don't know why, but I *can't* get sick at Granny's."

I slapped my cheeks and pinched them to give them color. Then I peered at my reflection in the mirror above the sink.

"Oh, great." I wasn't pale anymore. Now my face was red and blotchy. I didn't look healthier. I looked like I had a rash!

I tried splashing water on my face, but it didn't seem to help, either.

"Are you all right in there?" Granny's voice called from outside the bathroom door.

"Uh, yes, Granny," I replied. I put a big healthy smile on my face and opened the door.

"I'd better show you to your room," Granny said. "We'll need plenty of sleep, if we're going to fight that cold."

"Sleep. That's what I need." I bobbed my head in agreement. "I've been up since five. I'm beat."

Granny led me up the stairs to the second floor.

Show me my room and then leave me alone, I thought. I followed Granny into a small room under one of the eaves of the house. It was like a pirate's hideout. The headboard of the bed was painted with sailing ships. The dresser looked like a sea captain's trunk. And the wall was hung with fishing nets and a giant stuffed marlin.

"Cool room." I nodded my approval.

"I'm sure you'll be very happy here," Granny said, turning down the bedcover. "Just remember, if you do get sick"—she slowly turned her head to look at me—*"I know how to take care of you."*

Her lips curled into that wacko smile again.

Why did she keep saying that? How would she take care of me? I shuddered. She was really giving me the creeps.

Finally Granny left the room. I put on my pajamas and collapsed on my bed. All those hours with that weirdo watching me had stressed me out.

I want to sleep for the whole weekend, I thought. Until Mom and Dad get back.

But I couldn't sleep. Dad's warning kept running through my head. *"Don't get sick at Granny's. Whatever you do—DON'T GET SICK."*

"I won't get sick," I mumbled to myself. I pulled the covers up under my chin and stared at the peeling plaster on the ceiling. "I won't get sick."

I repeated those words over and over. Finally I drifted off into a restless sleep.

A beam of sunlight hit me in the face, and I shot up from the bed. "Morning already?" I exclaimed. "It can't be."

I tried to swallow. My throat was sore. I sniffed. My nose was running. I had chills.

"Oh, no!" I groaned. "I'm sick!"

Something moved in the corner of my room.

I froze.

Then a dark figure stepped out of the shadows. It slowly moved toward me into the light.

"Granny!" I gasped.

She stayed in my room. Spying on me.

Did she hear me say I was sick?

"Was that a sniffle?" she demanded with an evil glint in her eye. "Oh, Corey! Granny definitely heard a sniffle!"

4

"**A** sniffle?" I tried to disguise my stuffed-up, nasal voice. "Are you kidding? I'm as healthy as a horse."

I beat my chest with my hand. That started a coughing fit.

Granny watched with wide-eyed glee. "I knew it!" she cried, clapping her hands together. "I knew you were sick."

"No!" I choked out. "I just got something caught in my throat." I clutched at the neck of my pajamas, willing myself not to cough, sneeze, or even sniff.

"I'd like to take a look at that throat," Granny crooned, moving closer to my bed.

Today she wore a white short-sleeved dress, white stockings, and white shoes. She looked like a nurse. Except for her sicko grin and the wild look in her eyes.

I watched Granny stick her hand into the pocket of her dress and pull out a gray plastic tube. "Let's see if we have a temperature."

"We? What do you mean *we?*" I asked, trying to sit up.

Granny unscrewed the lid and shook the little glass thermometer. "Open wide."

"Wait. I don't have a—"

Too late. Granny shoved the thermometer under my tongue.

"Don't talk," she ordered. "And don't bite down on the glass. It could shatter in your mouth, and then you'd be in big trouble."

My eyes widened. I tried to hold the glass tube in place with just my lips.

Granny held up her wrist and studied the second hand on her enormous watch. That watch was so big, I could hear it ticking. I counted the seconds as they ticked by. One by one.

Don't have a temperature, my mind commanded. *Don't have a temperature.*

"All righty." Granny reached for the thermometer and slowly pulled it out of my mouth. She stared at the little red line and clucked her tongue.

My heart sank. "Wh-wh-what?" I stammered. "What is it?"

"You have a fever, all right. Just as I suspected. A hundred and two."

"No way." I put my hand to my head. It did feel warm. But not *that* warm. "Let me see that."

I dived for the thermometer, but Granny yanked it away. And I fell out of bed.

"Yeow!" First my hands, then my knees hit the floor.

Granny stood over me with her hands on her hips. "See? You're so sick, you're dizzy."

"I lost my balance, that's all," I argued, rubbing my sore kneecap.

"I'm going to have to start your treatment right away." Granny dropped the thermometer back into her pocket.

"It's just a bruise," I cried, pulling myself to my feet. "It will be gone in a few days."

"Granny's not worried about a little bruise," she said, backing away from me. "Granny has to do something about that nasty, *nasty* temperature."

Do what? I tried to remember what Mom did when I had a fever.

"I have just the thing to help you. . . ." Granny moved toward the little closet under the eaves. She put her hand on the doorknob. "In here."

25

What could possibly be hidden behind that wooden door? Something really terrible, I bet.

Granny slowly opened the closet, and a rotten smell filled the room. Oh, no! I covered my eyes, waiting for the worst.

"There!"

I spread apart my fingers and peeked. Granny was pointing to three shelves crammed full of blankets.

I let out a sigh of relief. Blankets? That's all? Just some smelly old blankets? I laughed out loud.

"What's so funny?" Granny spun around and stared at me. I instantly shut up. "A bad fever can make a kid act crazy," she said.

Crazy? I swallowed hard and tried to look normal. But I could feel my whole body getting warmer. Not from the fever—from fear.

Granny carefully scooped up a stack of green army blankets. "There's only one thing to do for a fever like that. Sweat it out."

"Sweat?" I was already hot. "Couldn't I just take a Tylenol?"

Granny turned. Her eyes were two shiny, gray marbles. I caught my breath. She looked like some kind of monster as she marched toward the bed. "Five or six of these wool blankets should do the trick."

"Wool!" I gasped. "Granny, wait! I hate wool. It makes me itch."

"Nonsense." She dropped the blankets on top of me.

"No, I mean it!" I said, trying to shove the blankets off the bed. "I break out in little red blotches if I even look at a wool sweater."

"Don't be such a baby." Granny pushed me back down on the bed. She quickly unfolded the first blanket and shoved the edges under the mattress on both sides of my bed.

"Granny, please stop!" I begged as the blanket pinned me to the mattress.

Granny smiled her sicko smile. "Wool is the very best thing for sweating out a fever," she told me. She yanked the blanket tighter across my body.

"Okay, you've had your fun." I chuckled as she draped another blanket across my body. "This is a joke, right?"

"A fever is no laughing matter." Granny jammed the ends of the second blanket under the mattress.

I tried to lift my arms. They were stuck to my sides.

I laughed a little harder. "Uh, Granny? I can't lift my arms."

Granny didn't answer me. She unfolded two more blankets, tucking them under the mattress. They were getting heavier and heavier.

I tried to bend my knee, but the blankets held me too tightly. I tried my foot. No go. I couldn't even lift my hand.

I was trapped!

"Granny, please." The blankets pressed down on my chest. I could hardly breathe. Still Granny Marsha piled on more blankets.

"Usually five is good," she said, bringing over another pile of moldy blankets. "But for a young man your size, I think I'd better go for ten."

Ten!

Oh, no! It was starting. The itching. First on my back. Then my arms. Then my legs. Then my whole body.

AAAAGH!

Little streams of sweat ran down my neck and back. It felt awful. And it didn't help the itching.

"Hot! Too hot," I moaned.

"Nine. And ten," Granny counted out. Then she clapped her hands together. "There. That should do it."

My lungs screamed for air. "Can't breathe!"

I tried to tilt my chin up. I had to get oxygen. "Granny—*please!*" I gasped. "I really—can't—breathe. Granny?"

No reply.

I turned my head frantically from side to side on my pillow. "Granny? Where are you?"

The room was empty. Granny Marsha had vanished.

I struggled to get up. But I was totally pinned to the bed.

Panic rushed through me.

I tried to kick my legs. I fought to move my arms. I slammed my head back and forth on the pillow. But the blankets wouldn't budge.

The more I flailed, the more exhausted I became. And the harder it was to breathe. Sweat gushed down the sides of my face. Air wheezed into my lungs in a slow painful squeak.

I was itchy, sweaty, and suffocating!

"Help!" I rasped. "Somebody! Anybody! *Get me out of here!*"

5

I kicked. I thrashed. I squirmed. Anything to loosen those blankets.

"Out!" I cried. "Let me out!"

Granny had tucked me in permanently. I was paralyzed, barely able to move any muscle below my neck.

"Arrrgh!" I fell back with my head against the pillow, exhausted from the effort. Sweat oozed out of my pores. My hair, my pajamas, my pillow—everything was soaked.

"Itch. I itch," I panted. The awful itching feeling covered me like tiny crawling bugs. I thrashed my head back and forth. The itching was driving me crazy. And I couldn't stand the feeling of being trapped under pounds of wool.

"No!" I groaned. "I have to get out of here!"

If I could slide my elbow out to the side of the bed, maybe I could work the blankets loose.

I clenched my teeth, trying to ignore the itch and the sweat. And the moldy smell. I focused on getting free. I wiggled my shoulders, back forth. Back and forth.

The heavy blankets were loosening. Just a little bit.

I pushed harder with my shoulders. "Back and forth, back and forth," I urged myself. I scrunched up my face, concentrating. The blankets really *were* getting looser and looser.

Could it be? Can I . . . ? Yes! It was working! I could move my arm.

Not a lot. But just enough to bend my elbow.

The blankets were so heavy. It was hard to move. With a grunt, I jammed my elbow into the covers. They moved.

All right!

Now, If I could just lower my fist, then I could push the blankets out from under the mattress.

Done!

I punched the blankets. Once. Twice. A couple of more punches and I'd be free.

I huffed and puffed from the effort. Sweat gushed down my forehead and stung my eyes. I squinted my eyes shut to keep it out.

Almost . . . Almost . . . Wait a minute.

What was that?

I froze, listening to footsteps outside my room.

Granny! She'll know I'm trying to escape. I straightened the covers and pulled my arm back into the bed. I lay as still as possible. My heart slammed into my chest.

"Please don't come in," I whispered. "Please . . ."

Bang!

The bedroom door swung open and hit the wall.

Granny stood in the doorway. She held a tray with a large plastic pitcher full of water and a glass. "How's my patient?" she crooned.

"Terrible!" I yelled angrily. "Get me out of here!"

She stepped back in mock alarm. "Well! We're a little testy this morning, aren't we?"

I wanted to wrap my ten itchy, stinky, hot wool blankets around her head. But I couldn't. I was stuck.

"I'm not testy," I said. I made my voice calm.

"I'm hot. I'm squashed flat. I itch. *And I can't stand it!*"

She set the tray down on the table beside my bed. "What you need is a nice big glass of water. Am I right?"

"Yes." I realized I was dying of thirst. "Give me a drink."

"Ah, ah, ah!" Granny held up one finger and shook it at me. "That was very rude!"

"Please, Granny," I said, forcing my mouth to curl into a smile. "May I please have a drink of water?"

"Of course you may when you ask like that." She grinned as she bent to untuck the blankets.

It seemed to take forever for Granny to carefully remove all ten blankets.

As soon as my right arm was free, I reached up and scratched behind my ear. Oooooh, that felt sooo good!

Then I scratched all over my head. And all over my body. "Thank you, Granny!" I moaned with relief. "You don't know how much better I feel."

"I told you the blanket treatment works," Granny replied with a satisfied smile. "But you wouldn't believe me."

"I believe you now," I gushed. "I believe you."

"Good. It's time to replace those fluids you sweated out." Granny poured a huge glass of water from the pitcher and handed it to me. "There you go. Drink every drop."

I didn't need any encouragement. I've never been so thirsty. I chugged the entire drink. The cool water felt good going down my sore throat.

When I handed back the empty glass, she poured me another full one. "Drink up," she instructed me.

"Okay." I took the glass and tilted my head back. This time I drank more slowly. I didn't feel quite as thirsty.

Granny never took her eyes off me. "That's a good boy," she murmured, nodding her head up and down. "Drink lots of water."

"Thanks, Granny," I said, giving her the glass again. "I think that should do it."

"Nonsense." Granny filled the glass a third time. "You're completely dehydrated."

I put my lips on the rim of the glass and pretended to drink, but Granny didn't go for it. "No cheating," she said sternly. "Drink that entire glass."

Her eyes narrowed to those little slits and I could tell she was serious. As I raised the glass, that weirdo smile crept across her lips.

I forced myself to choke down a third glass of water.

She poured me a fourth.

"Granny," I protested. "I'm going to burst. I don't have any room left for that water."

"Keep drinking." Granny folded her arms and stood next to the bed. "You haven't even had a full gallon."

A full gallon! What does she think I am, a car?

"Drink!"

"Okay. Okay." I turned my head slightly away from her and lifted the glass. This time I let half the water go down my throat. The other half I carefully squirted out the corner of my mouth. It dribbled down my neck into the shirt of my pajamas. They were already soaked anyway, so who cared?

It was better than exploding.

My hand shook as I handed the glass back to Granny. My stomach bulged out in front of me. And sloshed when I made the slightest move. I clutched my middle and groaned.

If Granny forced me to drink another glass of water, I'd throw up. Or worse. Reluctantly I turned my head to see how much water was left in the pitcher.

It was empty. What a relief!

I fell back against my soggy pillow. "I'm done," I gasped. "Finished."

Granny picked up the tray. "Good boy. I'll be right back with your vitamin C."

"Vitamins?" I guess I could handle that. They would be chewable and small. Little tiny pills shaped like Fred Flintstone or Shamu the Whale. I figured they would fit into my bloated stomach.

Suddenly I felt a strange tickle. It wasn't in my stomach. It was lower. Then the tickle turned to a sharp twinge. I squeezed my knees together under the blankets.

"Bathroom!" I announced to the empty room. That gallon of water had raced right through me. "I have to go to the bathroom."

The twinge was getting worse. I threw back the soggy covers, but before I could make a move, Granny returned. She was carrying another tray.

"Where do you think you're going?" she asked. Her perky voice didn't match her mean, cold eyes.

"I'm going to the bathroom," I said, wincing in pain. And boy, did I have to go!

"Oh, no you don't," she commanded. "You have to take your vitamin C first."

I looked for the little plastic bottle of vitamins on her tray, but there wasn't one. Only another large pitcher. This one held a bright orange liquid.

"Orange juice!" I cried. "No way!"

"Oh, yes." She poured a full glass and held it in front of my face. "First, you drink this entire pitcher. *Then* you can go to the bathroom."

6

My eyeballs bulged out of my head as I poured the orange juice down my throat.

I tried to swallow, but I gagged. The orange liquid exploded out the sides of my mouth. "Yech!"

"Drink it, Corey!" Granny insisted. "You can do it."

She slapped me on the back, and juice shot out of my nose.

"Oh, gross!" My pajama top was wet and sticky. And now—I *really* had to go to the bathroom. I mean *really, really* badly.

I crossed my legs tightly. My face squeezed into a grimace. I'm going to wet the bed, I thought in a panic. Sweat poured down my face.

"Granny," I begged. "Please, I don't think I can hold it another sec—"

"All gone!" Granny interrupted my pleas. She held up the empty glass. "That wasn't so bad, was it?" She crossed to the bedroom door and opened it. "Now you can go."

I bolted through the open door with my kneecaps pressed together. I half walked, half ran down the hall. "I'm not going to make it," I muttered. "I'm not going to make it."

I stumbled through the bathroom door and made it to the toilet just in time.

When I finished, I collapsed against the sink. Relief!

I caught a glimpse of my reflection in the mirror and gasped in shock. I barely recognized myself. My hair was greasy and damp. It stuck out in every direction. My face was pale. And I had little red blotches all over my neck and arms from the wool blankets.

"Granny did this to me," I gasped. I clutched the sides of the sink. "She's nuts!"

Now my breath started to come faster. The more I thought about Granny, the more panicked I felt.

She really was crazy!

I can't go back to that room, I decided. I've got to get out of here. I've got to call Mom and Dad!

I knew if I could just reach them, they'd come and get me. There was only one problem. The phone number was on the refrigerator. And the refrigerator was downstairs. To get to the stairs I had to pass my room. And Granny was still there.

I paced in a tiny circle, trying to decide what to do. After checking out my miserable reflection once more, I made up my mind. Time to make a run for it!

I cracked open the door. Good. The coast was clear.

I tiptoed into the hall. But just when I was about to make a dash for the stairs, Granny stepped out of my room. She stood with her hands on her hips, blocking my way.

"Going somewhere?" she asked. She was using that sickeningly sweet voice.

"Um, no, Granny," I replied meekly. "I was just going back to my room."

"I'm glad to hear that." Granny dropped her arms to her side. "Because Granny has something very special to show you."

"Oh, really?" Uh-oh, I thought. Now what? "What is it?"

Granny waved toward my bedroom. I took one step into the room and froze.

Sitting in the middle of the floor was a large metal and rubber contraption.

"W-what is that?" I stammered.

"It's a treadmill," she explained. "I made it myself."

That monster machine didn't look like any treadmill I had ever seen. It looked like a cross between exercise equipment and something from a torture chamber. It had an instrument panel with lots of dials. Metal wrist cuffs were attached to the rails. A head grip extended up from the front panel.

"Time for your workout!" Granny announced.

Time to get out of here! I thought.

"I just remembered something I left downstairs!" I yelled. I lunged for the door, but Granny beat me there. Before I could reach the handle, she slammed the door and plugged in her machine.

"You need exercise," she declared, flipping a dial. The rubber tread started to move. "To build up your strength."

"Um, thanks, but I don't really need a treadmill," I protested, inching toward the window. "I can just go for a walk outside."

"Oh, no, dear, that's not possible." Granny snapped open the wrist cuffs. "Your resistance has been lowered by your illness. If you go outside you'll catch another bug." She pointed at the treadmill. "Now, Corey, get on that machine."

No way was I going to let her strap me to that thing. I put my fists on my hips. "I'm serious, Granny. I can't stand those machines."

"You said you hated wool," she argued, moving toward me. "And look what good that did for you. You sweated out your fever."

"That's right." I backed away toward the opposite wall. "And now I feel great!"

Just to prove it I did a couple of jumping jacks. My hand hit a lamp and knocked it off the bedside table.

"See?" Granny said smugly. "There's no room in here for that sort of activity. Now be a good boy and get on the machine. It's time for your workout."

"I don't need a workout." I glanced around, trying to think of something—*anything*. "I'm too weak. In fact, I'm so weak I need to lie down."

I threw myself at the bed and tried to dive under the covers. But Granny was too fast.

"Oh, no, you don't," she said, catching hold of both my arms. Boy, was she strong. For such a little lady, she had a powerful grip.

She pulled me toward the treadmill. Before I could stop her, she had my wrists strapped to the handrails.

"If you stay in bed, you'll get weaker. You have to keep moving." She fastened the head grip around my skull and flipped up the treadmill dial. "Work that sickness out of your system."

The motor revved faster and I started walking.

"Left. Right. Left. Right." Granny Marsha counted out loud as she watched me.

She was like a drill sergeant. How could Mom and Dad ever think this monster was a sweet little old lady?

"Walk. Walk. Walk." Granny moved closer to the machine.

"What are you doing?" I huffed.

I couldn't see her because my head was held in place by that head grip. I could only stare straight ahead.

"I'm turning it up," Granny explained. "This isn't exercise. This is the warm-up."

She flipped the dial up high.

Suddenly I was stumbling forward, tripping over my feet, trying to keep up with the spinning treadmill.

"Faster, Corey!" she ordered with glee. "Faster."

My bare feet thumped against the rubber. Faster and faster. My heart thudded against my rib cage as I struggled to catch my breath. *Right. Left. Right. Left.* My feet were flying.

Five minutes. Ten minutes. The muscles in the top of my thighs burned. "Stop it, please!" I begged.

"Ten more minutes!"

Granny laughed. A bone-chilling, evil laugh. How could Mom and Dad have left me with this maniac? I squeezed my eyes shut. My lungs ached. My heart pounded in my ears, and little spots appeared before my eyes.

Then a sharp pain sliced through my side. I clutched at it with my right hand.

"Granny, please," I panted. "My side. It's—" I could barely gasp out the words. "I think I'm going to collapse."

No response.

"Granny?"

She was gone.

Or was she?

Was she still in the room, just watching me with those beady gray eyes and nasty grin? I hated not knowing.

I wrenched my head hard to the right to try to see if she was behind me. My head came out of the vise grip. I scanned the room. Empty.

I twisted my left hand free and then unhooked my other wrist. Luckily the straps were flimsier than they looked.

When I finally staggered off the machine, I fell to my knees, desperately sucking air into my lungs.

"I've got to get out of here," I wheezed. "Before she comes back."

I thought about my friends whose grandmas made them chicken soup or hot lemonade when they were sick. I never heard of their grandmas torturing them back to health. And that's what this was. Torture.

"She's crazy," I huffed, still out of breath. "A total nutcase." Call Mom and Dad, I told myself. They'll rescue me.

But to do that, I had to get the phone number from the refrigerator in the kitchen. Downstairs.

I pulled on my jeans. I decided not to waste time putting on my shoes and socks. I carried them with me to the door.

"Open the door and make a run for it," I whispered, running over my plan in my head. I always talked to myself when I was nervous. And Granny Marsha gave me plenty of reasons to be nervous.

Okay. I would throw open the door, turn to the right, and take the stairs. The kitchen was just to the left.

"Grab the phone number and find the phone," I murmured. "It's probably in the living room."

I listened for any sound in the hall. Nothing.

"Okay." I put my hand on the doorknob. I took in a deep breath for courage. "On the count of three. One. Two—"

I turned the knob and pulled.

But nothing happened.

I turned and yanked again. Harder.

"Oh, no!" I gasped. "I'm locked in!"

7

Bam. Bam. Bam.

I pounded on the door with my fist. "Granny Marsha? Let me out of here. Do you hear me? Let me out!"

I waited. No answer.

"The window!" I turned and bolted across the room. "I'll go out the window."

I threw back the curtain. My eyes widened in shock.

Bars! There were bars on the window. On the inside.

"I'm a prisoner!" I gasped.

Out. There had to be some way out of this room! Out of this crazy house! I raced for the closet.

Maybe there was a way out through the back wall. I threw open the door and tossed the remaining blankets onto the floor. The back of the closet was solid. No way out there.

Why would Granny lock me in?

And why would she have bars on her guest-room windows?

But this is stupid, I scolded myself. A waste of time. Nothing that has happened since I got to Granny Marsha's has made any sense.

I tried the door again, rattling the knob. I kicked the bottom of the door.

Clang!

"Yeow! What's that?" Pain shot through my foot.

I bent down to examine the door. Metal! It was made of solid metal!

"Oh, no," I whispered under my breath. Not only was I locked in, but there was no way I could break down the door.

My eyes searched the room. Another way. There must be another way out. The floorboards!

I flopped down on all fours and tried to dig my fingernails into the planks. But I had been kidding myself. I could scrape and dig until my fingernails bled. The floor was solid.

I leaped back to my feet and beat my fists against

the walls. They were solid, too. I dashed back to the window. I grabbed the bars and shook them. They wouldn't budge.

"I'm being held prisoner!" I moaned, pressing my back against the wall.

Why? Why would Granny do this to me?

And why would Mom and Dad leave me with this terrible woman?

Maybe I had done something wrong. I *was* a jerk in the car, but so was Meg. She complained more about the heat than I did. So that couldn't be it.

Maybe it was my last report card. I got all B's and one D in math. Dad was pretty upset by that. And so was Mom.

My eyes widened. Could this be my punishment for getting a rotten grade? I shook my head. No, they wouldn't be that mean. Or would they?

Maybe they didn't know Granny was a loony. But no—Dad had warned me not to get sick. I was so confused, I felt dizzy.

I paced in a circle around the room. My head was starting to throb. I rubbed at my temples and kept pacing. One thought pounded through my brain. "I have to get out. Before it's too late. Before she kills me."

I circled and circled the room, thinking and thinking.

My headache got worse. I squeezed my eyes shut,

trying to make it go away. Then I heard something terrifying.

Footsteps.

My eyes popped open. "Oh, no," I gasped. "Granny Marsha is coming back."

My heart knocked against my ribs. I could barely breathe. Granny was going to torture me again! I just knew it.

Hide! I frantically scanned the room. But where?

The door lock clicked and rattled. I scooted into the far corner of the room. I knelt down, my back pressed against the wall.

The door swung open and Granny's body loomed in the doorway. She looked more like a nurse than ever. In addition to the white uniform, she had pinned one of those starched nurse hats to her hair. She put her hands on her hips.

"What's the matter, Corey?" she demanded. "Why aren't you on the treadmill?"

"I, um, just got off," I replied in a shaky voice.

Granny was beside the machine in two strides. She felt the motor with her palm. It was cold.

She turned to face me. "You're not telling the truth." She shook her head sadly. "Granny doesn't like little boys who lie."

"I'm sorry, Granny," I murmured. "I didn't *just* get off the treadmill. I guess it was a few minutes ago."

Granny took two steps forward and gestured for me to stand. I leaped to my feet and cowered in the corner.

"Do you know what this makes Granny think?" She bent over and put her face nose-to-nose with mine.

"No." My voice sounded tiny and weak.

Her face twisted into an evil sneer. "I think you don't *want* to get better."

I shook my head back and forth. "No, that's not true."

"I think you *like* being sick." Her voice was low and threatening. "And that just won't do, Corey."

I tried to turn my head away from Granny, but she grabbed my chin and forced me to gaze into her beady eyes.

"Children who like being sick don't like it for long at Granny's."

8

"I don't like being sick!" I cried in a shaky voice. "I *do* want to get better."

Granny kept her face two inches from mine. She stared deep into eyes. I forced myself not to blink. After a few moments she narrowed her eyes into little slits. "Are you sure about that?" she demanded.

I bobbed my head up and down.

Her lips crinkled into a smile. "Good."

Whew! What a relief. Maybe now she'd leave me alone.

No such luck.

Granny jerked her thumb toward the treadmill. "Let's see you prove it. Get on there and run."

I didn't have much of a choice. I stumbled over to the exercise machine and climbed on. Granny strapped my wrists and head to the treadmill, then flipped the start switch. She didn't even let me begin slowly this time. She spun the dial all the way up.

"Yikes!" My feet whizzed out from under me. I scrambled to get my balance and clutched the side railings.

My feet flapped under me. I wasn't exactly running. More like falling forward.

Granny stood in the corner, her face twisted into her sicko smile. "Left! Right! Left! Right!" she commanded.

My thighs were sore from the last time I was on the machine. And pain shot through my side right away. I crumpled forward, clutching my waist with my hand. "Oh, no."

Just when I was certain I couldn't run another step, Granny stepped out of the shadows and flicked off the machine.

"You look a little wobbly," she declared, unstrapping me.

I was so out of breath I couldn't answer. I could only nod.

I staggered off the treadmill and perched on the edge of the bed, wheezing. Every muscle in my body shook.

"Why, Corey!" Grandma exclaimed, pointing at my quivering hands. "You're trembling. I'd better get the medicine."

"Medicine!" I stumbled back to my feet. What kind of medicine would Granny force on me? "No. Please. No medicine."

But Granny didn't listen. She rushed out of the room and returned with what looked like a large tube of toothpaste.

"This should do the trick." She set the tube on the table and slipped on a pair of thick rubber gloves.

"Wh-why are you wearing gloves?" I asked nervously.

"For protection," she replied. She unscrewed the cap of the tube. "This is strong stuff."

"So strong you have to wear gloves?" I asked. "Let me read the label."

"Label?" Granny threw her head back and laughed. It was not a pleasant sound. "There's no label. This is my own special medicine. Made from my own recipe."

Her own recipe? My insides did a flip-flop. Something really rotten had to be in that tube.

I glanced desperately at the door. If I could just get my legs to stop shaking, maybe I could make a dash for the kitchen. Then I could grab the number

54

for the hotel and call my parents. If I could just talk to them everything would be fine.

Granny squeezed a large greenish-yellow glop onto the finger of her rubber glove. A smell like moldy cheese filled the air. "We'll just smear this all over your body."

"Oh, no you won't. I won't let you," I protested, backing away from her.

Granny extended her glove. I couldn't let her put that stuff on me. I had to hide. But where?

My eyes darted back and forth. The closet! I'll jump in the closet and lock myself in.

"Come on, Corey. Take your medicine like a big boy." Granny grinned wickedly and walked slowly toward me.

"What's in it?" I asked, backing toward the closet.

"It's a secret," she whispered.

"But what does it do?" I groped behind my back, trying to find the doorknob.

"You'll find out." Granny snickered.

That was exactly what I was afraid of.

I was at the closet door. My hand fumbled for the knob.

Granny reached for me.

"No!" I clutched the doorknob and flung the door open. But when I turned, the shelves were packed with blankets again. There was no place to hide.

55

"Where do you think you're going?" Granny asked, cocking her head and smiling.

"Nowhere," I bluffed. "I was just looking for a pair of gloves for myself."

"You don't need gloves," she shot back. "Now, I want you to rub this ointment all over your body."

Granny wiped the blob of sticky goo on the palm of my hand. It looked like a green slimy slug. The stinky cheese smell was so strong, it knocked my head back. Tears stung my eyes.

"Okay. Okay. I'll—I'll do it." I held my hand as far away from my body as possible. "But tell me what it is first."

"No!" Granny snapped. "Stop asking questions and start rubbing."

I carefully wiped some of the sludge on my arm. Little electrical shocks rippled across my skin. "I wish you would tell me what this does," I complained, spreading the gross goo onto my skin.

"Keep rubbing," she insisted. She squeezed an even larger glob on my other arm. "It's something to get rid of those chills."

You're the one giving me chills, I thought. If I could get rid of *you*, I'd be just fine.

Granny continued to squeeze out more of the awful medicine. "This will keep you nice and warm on those long winter nights."

Winter? How long did she plan to keep me here?

"Here's some more medicine," Granny said, squirting a long green strand across my back. The pricks of electricity raced across my shoulders. "Rub it all in. That's a good boy."

The smell made me gag. It was worse than rotting garbage. Worse than my sister Meg's health-food drinks. I held my nose and breathed through my mouth.

With my other hand I rubbed the green gunk into my skin as fast as I could.

"Yuck, yuck, yuck," I mumbled as I spread the green slime across my skin. "I'm going to throw up."

Granny waited until I'd smeared that disgusting ointment all over my body, then she led me to my bed.

"I want you to take a nap," she ordered, flipping back the covers. "It's important that you get enough rest."

I climbed into bed. Then she tucked the covers under my chin and ruffled my gooey hair with her gloved hand. "Sleep is just the thing for you, young man," she cooed. "You've had a very hard afternoon."

Hard afternoon? I had just had the worst afternoon of my entire life!

Granny smiled at me. "I'm going to dispose of these gloves and clean up," she said, heading for the door.

I lay very still, watching her leave. The door clicked shut.

Hmm. Only one click.

Did she leave the door unlocked? Was it possible? Maybe Granny was so worried about the goop on her gloves that she really did forget to lock it.

I threw back the covers and tiptoed toward the door. "Please let it be open," I muttered over and over. "Please. Oh, please!"

Halfway across the room a floorboard creaked. I froze. Did Granny hear that?

I waited for a full minute. But she didn't come back.

I inched my way across the room. Slowly, carefully, I reached for the doorknob. I touched the cold metal.

But just as I was about to turn the knob, I felt something. On my arm.

A little stabbing sensation. It started with a tingle and moved up my back.

"Yikes!" I leaped away from the door.

The creepie-crawlie feeling spread to my legs and across my back.

I felt tingly everywhere. Like little needle pricks. Then itchy. Again.

Really itchy. All over. Much worse than when I was trapped under the wool blankets.

I wanted to scratch my legs. My arms. My chest. I was frantic.

What's going on? I ripped off my shirt and stared down at my body in horror.

"Oh, no!" I screamed. "Something horrible is happening to me!"

9

"**F**ur!" I shrieked. "I've got fur all over me!"

Thick green hair covered my toes and feet. It circled my legs and grew all over my stomach and chest.

My hands trembled as I reached for my forehead. "It's even on my face," I moaned.

I stumbled across the room to the mirror above the dresser. Raising my big furry body, I peered into the glass.

A huge, ugly bearlike creature with yellow teeth and green matted fur stared back at me.

"AAAIIIIEEE!" I leaped away from the mirror. That creature was me! And I had hair all over me.

On my face, my neck. My back. "It's everywhere. Everywhere!" I shouted. "Oh, gross!"

I beat at the coarse hair blanketing my arms. "Get it off! Get it off me!"

I pulled. I tugged. I tried to rip the fur off with my teeth. But nothing I did seemed to affect it. The fur wasn't fake. The thick green stuff had somehow sprouted from my skin. But how?

"The ointment," I gasped. "Granny's green slime did this to me."

Why? I wondered. Why would she want me to grow fur? I yanked at the fur on top of my head and two big tufts of green fluff came out in my hairy hands. The fur was the same color as Granny's stinky goo. "Why would Granny Marsha do this to me?"

I squeezed my eyes shut, remembering her words as she smeared the awful green gunk on my arms. *Something to take away those chills,* she had said.

A fur coat would do that. Especially one that covered me from head to toe. I put my hands to my hairy face. "Granny turned me into a monster!" I whispered.

But I couldn't waste time freaking out. I had to escape. My only hope was to get that telephone number off the refrigerator and call my parents. Then run for my life!

I lumbered to the door. My legs felt like tree trunks. Big and heavy. Maybe all that exercise did something to the muscles. I could hardly lift them.

I stared down at my thighs. Somehow they had swollen. They looked like two big furry inner tubes. Then I realized they were getting bigger! I could feel my skin stretching.

"Stop it!" I ordered. First my body had grown fur. And now this!

I tried to lift my big furry arm and reach for the doorknob. But my arms also blew up like balloons. "What's happening to me?" I cried.

I tilted forward to look at my body. Just trying to bend made me groan.

I couldn't even see my feet. My stomach was in the way. It was incredibly swollen. I looked like a big round ball with four fuzzy arms and legs sticking out the sides.

"I have to escape," I rasped. "Somehow!"

With a mighty effort I managed to heave one leg forward. I bent over my giant belly, trying to catch my breath.

Then I heard a squeaking sound. It was my

stomach, stretching. My big round gut was swelling again. Getting bigger. And bigger. I stared down at my stomach in horror.

"Stop!" I screamed. "If I get any bigger, I'm going to explode!"

10

~~~~~

I clutched my stomach. Shutting my eyes, I waited, helplessly, for the explosion. But nothing happened. I popped open one eye. Then the other. I patted my stomach gently.

It stopped growing.

Whew! I sighed, relieved.

I rested my hand on my stomach. It seemed to be getting smaller! It seemed to be shrinking!

I felt brave enough to glance down. The effort of bending over rocked me forward. I lost my balance and hit the doorknob.

"Ooomph!" The knob jabbed me hard in the stomach. Air rushed out of my mouth. As it did, my stomach collapsed even further.

My stomach really *was* deflating! I glanced over at my arms and legs. They were getting smaller, too.

All right!

I ran to the mirror to examine myself. I was normal-sized again. But the fur was still there.

I shuddered. How could that hideous monster be me?

"Mom," I whimpered. My chin quivered in the mirror. All of these weird changes were getting to be too much for me to take. "I wish Mom were here."

I was watching my eyes mist up when I remembered something. Just before my body had inflated I had discovered something. Something important.

What was it?

The door! That's right. Just before I grew fur, I thought Granny had left the door unlocked.

I didn't waste another second feeling sorry for myself. I turned toward the door and strode to it.

My hand touched the knob and gave it a twist. The door *was* unlocked. I pumped my first in the air and silently mouthed Yes!

Finally things were looking up. I opened the door slowly and waited, not daring to breathe.

No sign of Granny. Not a sound. Nothing.

Then ever so carefully I peeked my head into the hall.

Empty.

I took a couple of shaky breaths, then tiptoed out of my room. Every part of my body quivered. From excitement and fear.

All I had to do was walk down the stairs and into the kitchen, I told myself. A few seconds. That's all it should take.

It may have only taken a few seconds to get to the staircase, but it felt like a hundred years. My face was squeezed into a grimace as I tried to be absolutely quiet.

I took the stairs as quickly as I could.

I reached the bottom step.

Creak.

The wood groaned under my feet.

I froze. Did Granny hear that?

The floorboards squeaked above my head.

I closed my eyes, listening for Granny's footsteps. But the only sound I heard was my heart thundering in my ears.

Whew.

I gingerly stepped off the bottom step onto the downstairs carpet. I tiptoed toward the kitchen.

"Run to the refrigerator," I told myself. "Grab the number and dial."

I paused once more to make sure Granny wasn't coming downstairs. Then I bolted through the living room straight for the kitchen. In my mind I could see the slip of paper with Mom and Dad's number on it stuck under a little magnet mouse.

I'm going to make it! I'm going to make it!

Finally I reached the kitchen. I rounded the counter and lunged for the refrigerator.

I'm practically home!

The mouse magnet! There it was, clinging to the refrigerator door.

I stumbled forward. My hand reached out to snatch the note from under the mouse, but I suddenly stiffened. The mouse was still there. But the note from Mom and Dad had vanished.

"The number," I gasped. "The telephone number is *gone!*"

11

*G*one!

The note on the refrigerator. My parent's phone number! My only hope. Gone!

Frantic, I spun in a circle.

Where could it be?

I searched the kitchen. I flipped open cabinets. I checked the kitchen table and the counter by the sink. Nothing.

The horrible realization hit me. Granny must have taken the phone number. Or worse—thrown it out.

Thump. Thump. Thump.

Footsteps on the stairs.

Granny! She's coming. I quickly ducked below

the counter. And was about to scoot around the refrigerator into the dining room when I spotted something lying on the floor.

A piece of paper.

I held my breath and snatched up the paper.

With trembling hands I smoothed out the crumpled paper. There, in my mother's handwriting. The phone number!

I wanted to collapse on the floor with relief. But there was no time. Granny was coming.

I crawled into the dining room just as she entered the kitchen. Her rubber nurse's shoes squeaked across the linoleum.

I heard her open the refrigerator and pull something out of the freezer. She hummed as she plunked the food on the counter and then slid open a drawer holding pots and pans.

She's making dinner, I thought. Good. That should give me enough time to call Mom and Dad and get out of this house.

I crawled along the dining room rug into the living room. There was a phone there, but I didn't dare use it. Granny would hear me.

Granny's room, I told myself. She must have a phone in there.

Something clunked in the kitchen, and my heart pumped into high gear. Every bone in my body vibrated. It was now or never.

I turned and dashed through the living room. Granny's bedroom was just up the stairs at the end of the hall. I took the steps three at a time and flew down the hall. I raced past my room to Granny's. Her door was shut.

Please don't be locked, I begged silently. I reached for the knob.

The door swung open. For once luck was on my side!

A huge four-poster bed filled Granny's bedroom. The walls around it were covered with racks jammed with hats: straw hats decorated with plastic flowers and fruit, rain hats, and several spare nurse's caps. A trunk at the foot of the bed sat open. It was stuffed with what looked like medical supplies.

I recognized stethoscopes and glass beakers and rubber tubes. But I also noticed all kind of contraptions I had never seen before. I could only imagine what Granny would do with all of that equipment! It made my stomach turn to jelly thinking about it.

I better be quick. Before I discovered the hard way what those supplies were for!

Granny *did* have a phone. It sat on the little oak table beside her bed. Luck really was with me.

I tiptoed across the floor. A floorboard groaned and I froze. I strained to listen. Granny was still humming in the kitchen downstairs.

Perching on the edge of Granny's bed, I carefully unfolded the piece of paper. My hands trembled so hard I could barely read it. But there it was— Hampton Hotel, 555-3498!

I had just put my hand on the receiver when I heard another clunk. This one was real close. Right outside the bedroom door.

Oh, no!

Hide!

I dropped to the carpet and rolled under the bed, just as the door opened.

"Now, where did I put that rubber hose?" Granny murmured, striding across the floor to her trunk.

Rubber hose? Why would she need a rubber hose?

Granny's white nurse's shoes were only inches from my face. I could hear her as she rummaged through her medical supplies.

I held my breath, not daring to make a sound.

Please don't see me. Please don't see me.

"There you are!" she cried.

Oh, no, I thought. I'm caught! She's really going to punish me now.

I squeezed my eyes closed, waiting for Granny to drag me out from under the bed.

But nothing happened.

I opened one eye. Granny was pulling something

out of the trunk. It was the rubber hose. She hadn't seen *me* at all!

I grinned from ear to ear. *Still safe!* Granny strode out of the room, pulling the door closed behind her. I rolled out from under the bed and picked up the phone.

All I had to do was punch in seven little numbers, and help would be on the way.

I was so happy, I hummed as I dialed the number.

"One ring," I counted. "Two rings."

Click.

"Hampton Hotel," a woman's voice answered. "How may I help you?"

I smiled. This terrifying ordeal would soon be over. "Could you ring Mr. and Mrs. Ambler's room?"

"Ambler?" the clerk repeated. "Um, just a minute. Let me see."

I tapped my fingers on the table, waiting for the clerk to ring my parents' room. Hurry up, I urged silently.

"Ambler . . . Ambler," the clerk muttered. "Will you hold, please?"

I heard a click, and then I was listening to recorded music. When would my parents come on the line? Why was the clerk taking so long?

Thunk.

Was that a footstep in the hall? Was Granny coming back again?

No. Not now. Not when I'm so close to talking to my mom and dad.

The sound went away.

I was so nervous, I bounced off the bed. I hopped from one foot to the other.

Come on!

Finally the clerk came back. "I'm sorry, sir, but no one by that name is registered here."

"What?" I gasped. "They have to be. Did you spell the name right? Ambler? A-m-b-l-e-r."

"Yes, and I don't see it anywhere."

"But they can't have checked out," I insisted. "My sister's audition was today."

"They didn't check out," the clerk explained. "No one named Ambler ever checked in."

12

I stared at the receiver, stunned. Mom and Dad had never registered at the Hampton Hotel. What did that mean? Did they change their minds and go to a different hotel? Did Mom just forget to leave the right number? Or did she do it on purpose?

I felt dizzy.

Everything was so confusing.

"I don't understand. What is going on?" I mumbled. I dropped the phone on Granny's bed.

I stood in the middle of Granny's bedroom, completely stumped. I didn't know where to go. If I went back to my room, I'd be a prisoner again. And even if I could escape from Granny, how could I go outside? I looked like a monster.

I rubbed my face.

Wait a minute. Something had changed. I gazed at my hands. Skin! My skin was smooth. Then I glanced down. No more thick fur. There was regular skin everywhere.

"My body!" I squealed, pinching the flesh on my arm. "It's back."

I looked down at my stomach. No fur anywhere. "I'm normal!" I shouted. "I'm *me* again!"

I ran to the mirror hanging over Granny's dresser. My own face looked back at me. And not a trace of fur was left behind.

"Maybe I never had fur," I murmured. I put one hand to my forehead. Could I have had a fever? Did I just imagine the whole thing?

Then a terrible thought hit me. Maybe Granny put something in the water that made me crazy. "That's it!" I gasped. "I'm going crazy!"

Just the thought made the room spin. I clutched Granny's dresser to keep from falling over.

And that's when I heard it.

A voice. A muffled voice.

"Corey?" the voice whispered. "Corey, help me!"

I raised my head. "Oh, great," I groaned. "Now I'm hearing things."

"Corey!" the voice whispered again.

It was getting dark outside, and the light cast

weird shadows around the room. I narrowed my eyes and peered into the corners. "Y-y-yes?"

"Help me!" the voice pleaded.

I tried to say something. But no sound came out of my mouth. My throat felt as if a huge wad of cotton were stuck inside it. I tried to swallow.

"Corrrr-eeeeeee," the voice moaned.

My heart thumped like a drum. But I had to say something.

"Who—who's there?" I croaked.

"Help me!"

Someone—or some*thing*—was in trouble. I didn't want to help. I wanted to crawl under Granny's bed and hide. But I knew I couldn't.

"Please."

The plea sounded so desperate that I screwed together all the courage I had left and forced myself toward the voice. It sounded as if it were coming from inside Granny's closet.

Slowly. Slowly. I inched toward the closet door. I stuck out my hand.

What if something gross leaped out and grabbed me?

"Cor-eeeee!" the voice wailed.

I jerked my hand backward.

"Hurry!"

I yanked open the door.

Nothing.

Nothing in the closet but Granny's clothes. I shoved her dresses aside to peek behind them. Nothing.

"Corey. Over here."

The hairs on my neck stood up. I whirled around.

"Over *where?*" There was no place else to hide in Granny's room. I bent down and quickly checked under her bed. Nothing.

I peeked behind the coatrack. No.

"Come closer," the voice ordered.

Was it in the dresser? I yanked open the drawers. No. Where could it be?

"Corey—help me!" The voice was louder and more urgent.

I spun again. The voice wasn't coming from the closet, but someplace very close to it.

"Corey!"

I closed my eyes to concentrate. I followed the sound until my forehead touched the wall.

"Get me out of here!" the voice demanded.

My head jerked back. "I don't believe it," I gasped.

The voice was coming from *inside* the wall!

13

"**I**'m going crazy!" I announced to the empty room. "I'm delirious. First, I imagined I sprouted green fur. And now I'm hearing voices."

"Corey? Get me out of here, please!"

That was definitely a voice. And I definitely heard it. For real.

There was a small tear in the wallpaper. I tugged on it, and the paper slowly peeled away from the wall.

"That's it," the voice urged. "Keep pulling."

I yanked an entire strip off the wall and tossed it to one side. I glanced nervously at the door. Granny wouldn't like me messing up her wallpaper. Then I pulled another long strip of paper off the wall.

"Keep at it, Corey," the voice encouraged.

Now I was down to the plasterboard. It was old and crumbled like chalk. I dug at it with my fingernails. It fell apart in my hands.

"Faster, Corey," the voice pleaded.

I dug at the wall with both hands. I worked furiously. Sweat poured down the sides of my face.

"Faster!"

At last, I was able to make a hole in the drywall. It was about the size of a quarter. I bent down and peered through it.

"H-h-hello?" I stammered. "Is anybody there?"

A blue eyeball suddenly appeared in the hole.

"Yikes!" I leaped backward.

"Keep your voice down," the eye ordered. "And hurry up and tear the rest of this wall down."

I had never demolished a wall before. It was kind of fun. Until I thought about how much trouble I would get into when Granny saw what I had done.

But I planned to be long gone before she ever found out.

I hooked two fingers in the hole and pulled away a big chunk of plaster.

A hand on the other side of the wall did the same.

Then I grabbed an even bigger chunk of plaster. It tore away in a huge puff of white powder.

The chalk dust tickled my throat, and I clapped my hand over my mouth. I didn't dare cough or sneeze. The slightest noise like that would bring Granny rushing to the room.

With one hand still over my mouth, I grabbed the biggest piece of plaster and yanked it. Hard. White dust filled the air. I could barely see through it.

"At last!" the voice gasped from inside the swirling dust. "I'm free."

Someone stepped through the hole and into Granny's room.

I waved my hands at the white dust cloud, trying to make out who it was.

"Corey. Don't you recognize me?"

"Meg?" I couldn't believe it! "Is it really you?"

"Of course it's me." My sister swatted at the white chalk dotting her hair and shoulders. "Who else would leave the most important audition ever to try to rescue a dimwit like you."

She called me a dimwit. "Meg!" I cried. "It really *is* you!"

She still wore her black leotard and pink tights. Meg spit chalk out of her mouth. "Remember to keep your voice down," she warned. "Granny might hear."

I shuddered. "You know about Granny?"

"Why do you think I'm here? We thought you might be coming down with something." Meg smoothed a few stray hairs back into the tight bun on her head. "Dad warned you not to get sick at Granny's."

"It's not my fault," I protested. "I got the tiniest little sore throat, and *bam,* Granny turned into a maniac."

Meg nodded. "Granny Marsha used to be a nurse. In the army. But something happened."

"What?"

"Dad wouldn't say. But it was something *big.*"

I swallowed hard. "What does that mean?"

"It means I've got to get you out of here. And fast."

"You? What about Mom and Dad? Where are they?" I peered over her shoulder at the big gaping hole in the wall.

Meg frowned. "I'm not sure. I remember calling a taxi to bring me here. But I don't remember what Mom and Dad were going to do."

"I tried to call them, but the clerk said they never registered at the Hampton," I told her. "Did they switch hotels?"

"I don't know." Meg bit her lip. Then she shook her head impatiently. "What's wrong with me? I feel like there's fog in my brain."

So it wasn't just me. "It's this house," I explained. "It makes you crazy." I placed my hands on Meg's shoulders and pressed hard. She had to concentrate! I stared her right in the eyes. "Meg," I ordered. "Try to remember."

She screwed her eyes shut tight. "I *am.*"

"Let's start over. How did you get in the wall?"

My sister gazed over her shoulder at the hole we had just made. "The cab dropped me off out front," she began uncertainly. "I knew I had to hide from Granny Marsha, so I sneaked around to the back door."

"It was open?" I asked.

Meg shook her head. "No. The door was locked. But there was this little square hole with a rubber flap nearby."

"A doggie door?" I whispered. "I don't remember seeing a doggie door."

Meg put her hands on her hips. "Well, there *was* one, because I crawled through it. It was like this really long tunnel. And it led me here."

"A tunnel?" My heart pounded faster. Not from fear. From excitement. I had to force myself to keep my voice down. "You mean there's a tunnel leading from this room to the outside world?"

"Yes." Meg waved at the wall behind her. "That's it."

"Then what are we waiting for?" I cried. "Let's get out of here!"

"Wait!" Meg dug her heels in and wouldn't

budge. "We can't just jump back in there. We need a plan."

"Okay," I said quickly. "Here's the plan. We go through that hole, down the tunnel, and out the back door. When we hit the yard—we run for our lives." ·

I grabbed Meg's hand and dived through the hole in the wall.

It was pitch black in that tunnel. I couldn't see my hand in front of my face. I immediately walked straight into a wooden beam.

"Ouch!" I hunched over and grabbed the top of my head. "That hurt."

"Not so loud," Meg warned. "Granny will hear you."

"The ceiling is really low," I whispered as we hurried along the passage. "We're going to have to stay close to the ground."

"That's strange," Meg muttered. "I don't re-member having to duck before."

"Maybe you just did it automatically," I said.

"No." Meg grabbed my pajama top and pulled me to a stop. "I don't think we're going the right way."

I turned to face her. "You mean, there are *two* ways into the house?"

"There must be, if this is the *wrong* way," Meg replied in her snotty voice.

"Well, don't just stand there," I snapped. "Look for the right way."

"Don't talk to me like that," she shot back. "I mean, I did skip my audition to come back to help you, remember?"

"I know, I know, I know." I sighed. "But I'm really scared, Meg. If you and I don't get out of here quick, Granny's going to find us."

I could feel Meg shiver in the dark. "And we wouldn't want that to happen," she murmured.

"Right. Now let's find the right tunnel." I stuck out both hands and groped the darkness in front of me. My fingers touched wood beams, insulation, and wiring. All of it was covered with cobwebs. I didn't even want to think about spiders and bugs.

"Look! Here's something," Meg whispered.

I pressed myself closer to her. "I can't see anything."

"Do you feel it?" she said. "The draft?"

I felt a cool breeze against my face. I held out my hand. Nothing. I reached farther. Still nothing. I took a step forward and realized I was standing in a new corridor.

"It's another tunnel!" I cried.

"What are we waiting for? Let's take it."

I followed Meg this time. But this ceiling was even lower than the other one. We didn't just have to duck. We had to crawl on our hands and knees.

"This isn't it, either," Meg moaned. "I know I didn't come this way."

"Just keep moving forward," I urged. "Maybe there's more than one way out."

Then I realized something was very wrong. The floor beneath my feet suddenly changed from hard wooden planks to something really soft and mushy. The air in the tunnel smelled like a gross diaper pail.

"P.U." I squeezed my nostrils closed and crawled more slowly. I could only use one hand to help me move along, since I was pinching my nose with the other.

Whatever I was touching felt familiar. Like hair. Furry hair.

I put my knee down again and something squished under me. The stink got even worse. I shifted my hand and felt something crunch under it.

"Meg!" I whispered into the darkness. "What are we crawling on?" But I already knew. . . .

14

"**M**ice!" Meg squealed in horror. "We're crawling on dead mice."

I fell sideways, landing on a pile of furry bodies. Their bones snapped and popped beneath my weight.

"Yuck!" I put my hand down. Then my knee. "Oh, gross. Gross!"

I tried to leap to my feet, but the ceiling was too low. Meg did the same. She clutched at me in the darkness and scrambled up my back. "Get them off me, Corey. Get them off!"

"I can't, Meg," I replied. "They're everywhere!"

"Oh, Corey," Meg moaned. "I'm going to throw up."

I was stuck on my hands and knees, with Meg lying across my back. She wasn't going to allow any part of her body to touch that carpet of dead mice.

For a skinny ballerina she seemed to weigh a ton.

"Corey, I mean it!" Meg wrapped her arms around my neck in a stranglehold. "Get me out of here—now!"

I was up to my wrists in mice. I tried to crawl forward, but after a few feet my head hit a wall. "Dead end," I choked out. "We've got to go back."

"Over all of those mouse bodies?" Meg moaned. "Never!"

"We have to." I bucked Meg off my back with a sudden jerk. "And we will go a lot faster if we each go on our own."

"Ew! Ick!" Meg whimpered as we crawled back across the carpet of mice. "I hate this, Corey. I really hate it!"

I tried not to think about the little tails and feet squishing through my fingers and snapping under my knees. I just concentrated on getting back to a wood floor and finding another passage out.

We crawled for a few more minutes, turning right, then left. Then right again.

"Light!" Meg cried suddenly. "I see light."

"I see it, too!"

I half crawled, half ran toward the yellow glow in

87

the darkness. We left the mouse bodies behind and were finally on a hardwood floor.

Meg clutched my arm. "The light's getting closer. We're almost there."

As soon as we could stand up, we took off running.

"I see a door!" I rasped.

"I do, too!" Meg cried.

Yellow light streamed from under it. All we had to do was throw open that door, and we'd be home free.

"Outside!" I cried. "Here we come!"

Meg burst through the door first. I was right on her heels. I stumbled forward with my arms outspread like a runner breaking the ribbon at the finish line.

"We made it!" I gasped. "Made . . ."

My words died in my throat as I realized where we were.

"No!" Meg screamed.

We weren't outside.

We had run through Granny's closet door.

We were back in Granny's room!

15

The bedroom door banged open and Granny stalked in. She wore a complete nurse's outfit—white dress, little starched cap, white shoes—and now she'd added a navy blue cape. Bright red lipstick was smudged crookedly across her wide mouth. Her gray hair frizzed out wildly from under her cap.

She looked totally insane.

"Time for your fluids!" Granny chirped, giving us both a big smile. She didn't seem at all surprised to see Meg.

"Fluids?" Meg's eyes were two big round circles.

"I brought two gallons." Granny held up her tray

stacked with pitchers and glasses. Oh, no! Not again! "One for Corey. And one for Meg."

I gaped at Granny. How could she have known Meg was here?

Granny kicked the door shut behind her, then carefully set the tray on the bedside table.

"Time for sick little children to take their medicine!" Granny giggled, giving Meg her warped smile.

"But I'm not sick!" Meg protested.

"Now, Meggie, look at yourself." Granny put one hand on my sister's forehead. "You're very hot."

"That's because I've been running," Meg replied.

"Running a fever, more likely. But don't worry, dear." Granny picked up one of the pitchers and showed it to Meg. "Granny will take care of you. Granny takes care of everyone."

"Don't drink a drop," I warned my sister. "It'll make you crazy."

"A gallon of this ought to set you on the road to recovery," Granny said. She filled two glasses with water.

"I'm not drinking a gallon of anything!" I yelled at Granny.

"Now, Corey, you're just being difficult," Granny scolded. She approached me slowly. "You know that won't make you better. And you want to get better—don't you?"

She thrust the water glass toward me, but I ducked under her arm.

"Run, Meg!" I yelled from behind Granny.

"Where?" Meg cried. Before she could move, Granny grabbed hold of her wrist. "Ow! She's got me."

"You're as bad as little Corey," Granny declared, shoving the glass of water up to Meg's lips.

"Grit your teeth!" I shouted at Meg. "Don't let Granny get your mouth open!"

Meg shook her head back and forth. She locked her jaw. And no matter what Granny did, she couldn't get Meg to open her mouth.

Granny slammed the glass on the table. "I told you this was no time for games," she snarled. "Since you won't open your mouth for Granny, Granny will have to open it for you." She came at Meg with both hands outstretched.

"Help! Corey!" Meg screamed as she backed into the corner. "Get her away from me."

Granny grabbed Meg's arms and pinned her roughly against the wall.

That did it!

I grabbed one of the pitchers from the table and raised it above my head. "You let Meg go or I'll hit you with this!" I shouted.

Granny turned to look at me. When she saw the

91

pitcher full of water, she froze. There was major fear written all over her face.

I stared at the water and back at Granny.

She looked just like the Wicked Witch in *The Wizard of Oz.* That made me think of something. I suddenly remembered the final part of the movie when the Witch cornered Dorothy and her friends. They were trapped and the Witch had just set the Scarecrow on fire with her burning broom.

"Water," I whispered. "Water melted the Wicked Witch."

"No." Granny went pale with fear. "No water."

Granny stayed frozen, staring at the pitcher I held in my hand.

I clutched the pitcher tighter. Maybe, just maybe, the water would melt Granny.

Granny never took her eyes off that pitcher. "Be a good boy, Corey," she cooed sweetly, "and put down that pitcher."

"No!" I glared at her.

Granny still gripped Meg's arms. She inched closer to me, dragging Meg with her. "Come on, Corey, hand it over."

"Never!" I shouted.

Then Granny lunged. I took one step back and hurled the water at her.

"Oh, no!" Granny shrieked. She let go of Meg and tried to protect her head. The water soaked her head and hands. I grabbed the second pitcher and doused her with that, too.

"Yeow!"

She howled as if she'd been sprayed with acid.

Water dripped down the side of her face and soaked her body. Every spot it touched made Granny Marsha squirm in agony.

Meg ran around Granny and cowered behind me. We stared at Granny, waiting for her to melt.

We waited. And waited.

Granny kept on squirming and crying.

But nothing else happened.

Then Meg looked at me. And I looked at her.

Why wasn't Granny melting?

16

"**D**o something!" Meg ordered, jabbing me in the back with her elbow. "Make her go away."

I had already thrown two full pitchers of water all over Granny Marsha. The only thing left on the tray was the glass of water she had tried to force down Meg's throat. I grabbed it and poured it directly on top of her head.

Suddenly Granny's eyes grew huge. The drops of water spread across her forehead, then ran down her face to her chin.

Her mouth opened, but no sound came out.

I watched in awe as little blisters popped up wherever the trails of water had trickled.

"Corey, what's happening?" Meg cried, digging her nails into my arm.

The blisters on Granny's face got bigger and bigger.

"I'm melting," Granny wailed as her body caved in on itself. "Melting."

Wow. Just like in the movies.

Only this time it was real.

Meg and I stood completely frozen, hypnotized by the horrible sight.

"Unngh." Granny bent forward at the waist, then lifted her face to look at me.

Pure hatred gleamed in her eyes.

"How could you?" she screeched.

Foul breath blasted into my face, and I grimaced.

"Her face!" Meg gasped. "Corey, look at her face!"

The blisters on Granny's face had swollen into each other. They had somehow all joined together.

We watched her whole forehead bulge out in a gigantic bubble. Then it drooped forward like a big blob of melting candle wax.

"Oh, yuck," Meg groaned.

"Stop!" Granny screamed. Her nose grew longer and longer, stretching down past her chin.

"Stop thissssssssss!" she cried as her lips warped out of shape.

"Oh, gross." I leaned back into my sister.

"Meeeellllttttiiiinnnnng." Her voice sounded like a tape that was going too slow.

But most disgusting of all were Granny's beady gray eyes. They shot out of their sockets and dangled from the blobs of melted skin dripping off her chin.

"AAAARRGGGGH!" Meg and I screamed together.

Granny's head melted into one huge, awful glob.

Now Granny was swaying from side to side. I stared, horrified, as her head and then her body collapsed into a short, square lump in a nurse's uniform.

"Stop. Stop," Granny wailed. "You rotten little creatures. How could you? How could you?"

Meg covered her ears with her hands to block out Granny's shrieks. But she didn't cover her eyes. It was too amazing a sight to miss.

Then Granny's head totally dissolved into her body, and we could no longer hear any words. Just a low moaning.

The lump that used to be Granny oozed into a puddle of green and brown sludge that oozed across the floor.

"Look out!" I cried, pulling Meg out of the slime's path. "Don't let it touch you."

We pressed our bodies against the bedroom wall

as it slithered past our feet. Finally the ooze stopped spreading.

Meg and I gazed at each other.

We were safe.

But not for long.

Hisssssssss.

A thick cloud of steam billowed into the air. The stench was awful, worse than rotten eggs, worse than the tunnel of dead mice we crawled through.

"Gross!" I covered my mouth with my hand.

Meg buried her nose in my back. "I'm going to throw up. I'm going to throw up!"

I pinched my nose closed. "Just keep telling yourself, Granny's gone. The witch is gone," I ordered in a nasal voice.

Meg raised her head to peer over my shoulder. Tears filled her eyes. "You did it, Corey, you did it!"

"Hooray!" I pumped my fist in the air.

Then I heard a weird sound. Like soda pop fizzing.

The fizzing got louder. And louder. It sounded like a thick, bubbling liquid.

"It's hot!" Meg suddenly moaned. "Why is it so hot in here?"

Meg was right. I could feel the heat on the back of my neck. Like a white-hot furnace, blasting me.

I spun to see what was happening.

The walls glowed red. They looked like coals

turning from orange, to blue, to white as they got hotter and hotter.

"Don't touch anything," I ordered. I dragged Meg away from the wall.

Meg covered her face with her hands and stood as close to me as she could. "Corey, make it stop!"

"I can't!" I cried, watching the walls melt.

The wallpaper peeled off in big strips that turned to syrupy dribbles spreading across the floor. It glowed like hot lava as it streamed toward the puddle that used to be Granny.

Another blast of sulphurous steam shot in the air as the ooze hit the puddle.

"The door!" I choked out. My eyes burned from the heat and the terrible chemicals in the air. "We've got to get out."

I half carried, half dragged Meg toward the door. As we passed the bed, the headboard split in two and melted to the floor. Then the mattress curled up like a ball of plastic that had been set on fire. It oozed all over the sides of the frame and disappeared into the bubbling glop.

The wooden floor rolled under us in waves.

"Whoa. Look out!" I yelped. Meg and I staggered to the right, trying to avoid touching the walls or any of the goo. Then the floor bucked us back to the left.

"What's happening?" Meg screamed.

"The floor," I groaned. "The floor is warping from the heat."

"Corey, no!" Meg wrapped her arms tighter around my waist. I could barely catch my breath.

"The door. We have to get to the door," I gasped, stumbling over the heaving floor.

But just as I reached the door, it burst into a stream of sizzling ooze.

Everywhere I looked—the walls, the bed, the dresser, everything was turning into boiling lava.

"The room!" I shrieked. "The whole *room* is melting."

We were surrounded by bubbling ooze.

"What do we do, Corey?" Meg wailed as the floor finally became part of the river of red. "Where should we go?"

I was paralyzed. I couldn't move. I could barely talk.

"Nowhere," I whispered. "We're trapped. We're going to be destroyed with the house!"

17

"**C**orey?"

I heard a voice in the distance and managed to lift one eyelid. A woman with blond hair and glasses stood over me. She held a glass of water in one hand.

"No!" I croaked. My throat was bone dry. My lips were parched. "No more water."

The woman smoothed my hair back from my forehead. "Calm down, Corey. It's me—Mom."

I blinked several times. The room seemed to tilt a little. "Mom? Is it really you?"

My mother smiled and nodded.

"And is this my room?"

"Of course it is, honey. You're safe and sound in your own home."

For the first time in days I smiled. A huge ear-to-ear grin of relief.

"Jack?" Mom called over her shoulder. "Corey's waking up!"

"That's great," a deep voice replied.

I heard heavy footsteps. Then another face came into focus next to Mom's. The face was smiling.

"How are you doing, champ?" Dad squeezed my hand.

"Not so hot." I tried to pull myself to a sitting position.

Dad placed one hand on my shoulder and gently pushed me back down on the bed. "Lay back and relax. You've had a rough couple of days."

"I'll say," I rasped. "Granny Marsha is evil."

Mom and Dad glanced at each other. "Granny Marsha?" Mom said. "Who's that?"

Dad shrugged. "I don't know."

"You know Granny Marsha!" I cried, lifting myself up again. "She's your mother, Dad! Come on, don't joke."

Dad looked at Mom. "I don't have the foggiest idea what he's talking about."

Mom knelt next to the bed. "Corey, you know your grandmother's name is Betsy."

"Betsy?" I repeated.

"Of course. Grandma Betsy. She lives right next door." Dad patted me on the shoulder. "Boy, it sounds as if you had one whopper of a bad dream."

"Dream?" I frowned. "But—but it seemed so real."

"Fever dreams can be very vivid," Mom explained. "And upsetting. Thank goodness the fever broke."

I put my hand to my head. "Did I have a fever?"

"A hundred and six degrees," she replied. "You were delirious."

Dad sat on the edge of my bed. "You've been out of your mind for several days."

"Wow." I fell back against my pillow. "Everything was so real. Especially that woman." I shivered. "Granny Marsha."

Mom handed me the glass with the straw in it. "Drink this. We need to get some liquids back in you."

"That's what Granny Marsha said," I muttered. The effort of sitting up and lying down and sitting up again had worn me out. The room started to spin, and Mom's face got blurry. "She made me drink gallons of the stuff."

Mom set the glass on the table next to my bed. "Well, don't worry, I'm not forcing you to do anything."

Dad patted my hand. "You get some rest. It's the best thing for you."

I turned my head toward the window. Beams of bright sunlight hit my face. I smiled happily. Home. I thought. I'm home.

I turned back toward my dad, and my smile faded from my face.

He was gone. And in his place was a face I hoped I'd never see again. In real life or in my dreams.

Granny Marsha! Holding a huge pitcher of water.

18

"No! You're not real!" I shouted. "You're not real! You can't be!"

Granny Marsha felt my forehead, and her disgusting breath washed over my face. "Still warm, I see. We're going to have to do something about that."

"No!" I batted her hand away from me. "You're a fake. Dad said so. You're just a bad dream. You don't even exist."

"Take it easy, Corey," Granny Marsha cooed. "You were having a nightmare. But you're okay. You're still here—safe and sound in Granny Marsha's house. And I think you need more medicine. I'll go get some for you right now."

I covered my head with my pillow. "No! Nooo!" I yelled into the mattress.

I kicked my feet hard on the bed. "Go away!" I screamed under the pillow. "I don't want to see you."

It was hot and dark under the pillow. I was running out of air. Drool dribbled from my mouth onto the mattress, making it soggy. Little dots of yellow and purple swirled in front of my eyes.

I threw the pillow off my head and flipped over onto my back. I gasped for air, sucking big breaths into my lungs. My eyelids flew open. And for one second I didn't know where I was.

I scanned the room. I saw a ceiling with a bright overhead light. White cupboards with little brass knobs. A wooden table leg and wooden chairs. In the background I could hear the final notes of the song "Over the Rainbow" coming from the television.

It didn't seem like Granny Marsha's house. But I had to be sure.

I tilted my head, ever so slightly. And sniffed.

The rotten-smelling breath was gone. That meant Granny was gone!

But wait a minute. My room was gone, too.

Even my bed had vanished.

My face was resting against something cool and hard. Linoleum tile. I was lying on the black-and-white linoleum floor of our kitchen.

A large face appeared in front of me. "Hey there," the face said.

Meg!

She cocked her head to smile at me. Then she stretched out one hand and patted me on the stomach.

I flipped over onto my side, and she scratched behind my ear. I liked that.

"Mom, he's awake," Meg called over her shoulder.

A pair of feet padded across the kitchen, and another face appeared next to Meg. It was Mom. She reached out and patted me on the head.

"Wow!" Meg said. "He must have had one bad dream. Did you see him? All four of his legs were moving like crazy. And he was barking and whining in his sleep."

I was still a little woozy. I continued to lie still on the floor while Mom smoothed the hair over my shoulders. "Poor Corey. Poor little doggie. Ever since we moved to Fear Street, he's been having these horrible dreams. Sometimes three, four times a day."

"I wonder what a dog dreams about?" Meg asked.

Mom shrugged. "Maybe he's chasing rabbits."

Meg tilted her head to look at me. "I wouldn't think rabbits would get him that upset. He was really whimpering."

I raised my head groggily. This was definitely home. My kitchen. My floor. My humans. I could even see my food dish on its little plastic mat by the back door. Everything else had just been a terrible nightmare.

"You don't need to be afraid of a little old rabbit," Meg cooed, wrapping her arms around my neck. "You're a big doggie."

I was really happy to see Meg. And just to prove it, I stuck out my tongue and licked her cheek.

"Oh, ick, Corey." Meg giggled, drying her face with her sleeve. "Dog kisses."

I knew she liked it. And I thumped my tail to let her know I knew.

Boy, was it good to be back in the real world. Everything back to normal. I stood up and stretched. I had a big day ahead of me.

First I'd have a drink of water and maybe a little dog chow. Then later I'd chase that rotten cat with the slate-gray eyes. She hangs out in the deserted house on the other side of Fear Street.

"Maybe today . . . I'll catch her!"

Are you ready for another walk
down Fear Street?
Turn the page for a terrifying
sneak preview.

R•L•STINE'S

GHOSTS of FEAR STREET ® #17

HOUSE OF A
THOUSAND SCREAMS

Coming mid-January 1997

What was that creak? Was the ghost sneaking up on us now? If it could make dress dummies and bedspreads come to life and attack us, what else could it do? Could it take over our parents? Control them? Make them wander through the house like robots?

I shuddered and burrowed further into the covers. Something hard poked my arm. I felt around and found the object. I peered at it in the dark.

Uncle Solly's magic glasses—the ones we saw the ghost with—lay next to me in my bed!

But I'd left them in my room! I clearly remembered putting them down on my dresser. Right before I went to brush my teeth.

"Freddy?" I called softly.

No answer.

"Freddy, wake up." I reached up and gave him a shove.

"What?" He sat up, rubbing his eyes. "What is it? What?"

"The magic glasses," I said urgently. "Did you bring them in here from my room?"

Freddy leaned down from his bunk and grabbed his own glasses from the nightstand. "No."

"Well, why are they in my bunk, then?" I felt panic rising again, grabbing me by the throat.

The glasses had moved on their own!

"Maybe the ghost put them there," Freddy suggested.

Maybe. But why?

I slipped the glasses on and looked around the room. No poltergeist. *Whew!*

Then I heard another noise from downstairs. A new noise. The sound of something scraping, shuffling against the floor.

Something was down there. I was certain of it. Was it the ghost planning to get me and Freddy? Or Mom and Dad?

Stay calm, I told myself.

Yeah, right.

I pushed back the covers and climbed out of bed. "Get up," I ordered Freddy.

We couldn't just lie there in the dark waiting for whatever it was to come get us. We had to *do* something.

Even if it meant risking our lives!

We needed weapons. The best we could come up with was Freddy's baseball bat and my tennis racket. Oh, well, better than nothing. Holding them ready, we tiptoed down the hall.

I still had the magic glasses on. So I spotted him right away. The little ghost from the attic. Leaning calmly against the stair railing. He looked as if he was waiting for a bus.

I jumped forward and swatted at him.

He vanished! Just like that!

I spun around. "Where'd he go?" I asked softly.

"Peeps," I heard in my ear.

"Ack!" I squawked. "Freddy! The ghost! He's on my shoulder!"

"Hold still!" Freddy ordered, and swung the bat.

I barely ducked in time to save my head. "Watch it, lamebrain!" I whispered furiously. "You almost decked me."

"I didn't mean to," he argued. "I can't see the

stupid ghost, remember? You're the one wearing the magic glasses. I was just trying to help."

I reached up and felt my shoulder. Nothing there.

"Well, he's gone, anyway," I said. "That's what matters. Now, for Pete's sake, keep quiet. The last thing we need is for Mom and Dad to wake up and catch us out here. They'd ship us to the loony bin for sure."

We crept down the stairs. The ghost kept popping in and out of sight. Each time, I took a swing at him with my racket. And missed.

He was playing with us! The little creep!

When we reached the downstairs hall, the ghost stood on a chair. Waiting for us. His little black eyes glittered at me. I pounced and thwacked the racket on the seat of the chair.

Nothing.

"Did you get him?" Freddy asked.

"No," I growled. I flipped on a light.

"How come you keep missing?" Freddy wanted to know.

I gave him a look. "He keeps vanishing. How do you expect me to hit something that can just blink on and off like that? I think he pops from one place to another."

Then I heard *"Peeps"* again. And felt something land on my head. Oh, yuck! A ghost on my head!

I slowly raised my hands, trying to catch the little guy by surprise. All I caught was air.

Frustrated, I pulled off the glasses and handed them to Freddy. "Here, you try. Maybe you can do better. And use my racket instead of that bat. That way at least you won't kill *me* while you're trying to bean *him.*"

Freddy leaned the bat against the wall and gave me his glasses to hold. Then he put on the magic glasses.

"There he goes!" he called immediately. He sped toward the den. I followed.

When I got there, I found Freddy standing still as a statue. The light was on—his hand was still on the switch. The tennis racket hung loose in his other hand.

All around us was that weird little sound: *"Peeps. Peeps. Peeeeeeps!"*

I felt cold. "What's going on?" I said. "Freddy, what's wrong?"

Silently, he handed me the glasses. I slipped them on.

And gasped.

The room was filled with tiny ghosts!

They sat on the bookshelves, and the television.

They hung from the lamps, from the ceiling fan. They danced along the curtain rods. They bounced on the sofa cushions.

There were *dozens* of the little guys. And all their vocal cords were working overtime. *"Peeps. Peeps. Peeeeps!"*

Then, all at once, every single one of them stopped peeping. And turned to face us.

Slowly, they made a circle, surrounding us. My knees shook so hard I thought I was going to fall over. I reached out and grabbed the back of a chair.

"Wh-why is it quiet all of a sudden?" Freddy stammered. Without the magic glasses, he had no idea what was going on. "What's happening?"

"You don't want to know," I told him. "Just stick close to me."

The ghosts' black eyes gleamed. The circle closed tighter. And they drew nearer.

Nearer.

This was the end! I shut my eyes. I didn't want to see.

Then a new sound broke the silence. A much uglier sound than the ghosts' peepsing. It snarled and rumbled like nothing I'd ever heard.

My eyes flew open. I spun around, trying to see what it was.

Then I realized the sound came from outside the room.

But whatever made it was moving toward the den.

With a mad burst of *peepsing,* the ghosts scattered. One leaped to an electric socket. I gasped as his body thinned, folded like paper, and squeezed through the tiny plug hole.

Others slipped like mist through cracks in the brick chimneypiece. One flattened itself and slid under the closet door. In a flash they were gone. We were alone.

The snarling noise grew louder. Clearly, whatever made that horrible sound had scared away all the ghosts.

And if it could scare a ghost, what kind of horrible thing could *it* be?

Without realizing it, Freddy and I had backed up all the way to the wall. Our backs were against it when a solid *thud* came from the other side. I could feel it all down my back.

Whatever was on the other side of that wall was powerful. And it was *coming after us!*

A horrible, bubbling growl ripped the air.

"We've got to get out of here," I whispered.

Freddy didn't answer. He simply barrelled out of the room.

"Wait for me!" I called, and tore out behind him.

We rushed up the stairs and into Freddy's room. I closed the door and turned the key in the lock.

"That should do it," I said. I moved into the room.

Freddy stared past me. "Look!" he whispered hoarsely. He pointed at the door.

I looked.

The doorknob was turning. All by itself.

About R. L. Stine

R. L. Stine, the creator of *Ghosts of Fear Street,* has written almost 100 scary novels for kids. The *Ghosts of Fear Street* series, like the *Fear Street* series, takes place in Shadyside and centers on the scary events that happen to people on Fear Street.

When he isn't writing, R. L. Stine likes to play pinball on his very own pinball machine, and explore New York City with his wife, Jane, and fifteen-year-old son, Matt.

R·L·STINE'S
GHOSTS of FEAR STREET®

1 HIDE AND SHRIEK 52941-2/$3.99
2 WHO'S BEEN SLEEPING IN MY GRAVE? 52942-0/$3.99
3 THE ATTACK OF THE AQUA APES 52943-9/$3.99
4 NIGHTMARE IN 3-D 52944-7/$3.99
5 STAY AWAY FROM THE TREE HOUSE 52945-5/$3.99
6 EYE OF THE FORTUNETELLER 52946-3/$3.99
7 FRIGHT KNIGHT 52947-1/$3.99
8 THE OOZE 52948-X/$3.99
9 REVENGE OF THE SHADOW PEOPLE 52949-8/$3.99
10 THE BUGMAN LIVES! 52950-1/$3.99
11 THE BOY WHO ATE FEAR STREET 00183-3/$3.99
12 NIGHT OF THE WERECAT 00184-1/$3.99
13 HOW TO BE A VAMPIRE 00185-X/$3.99
14 BODY SWITCHERS FROM OUTER SPACE 00186-8/$3.99
15 FRIGHT CHRISTMAS 00187-6/$3.99
16 DON'T EVER GET SICK AT GRANNY'S 00188-4/$3.99

Available from Minstrel® Books
Published by Pocket Books

Simon & Schuster Mail Order Dept. BWB
200 Old Tappan Rd., Old Tappan, N.J. 07675

Please send me the books I have checked above. I am enclosing $_____(please add $0.75 to cover the postage and handling for each order. Please add appropriate sales tax). Send check or money order--no cash or C.O.D.'s please. Allow up to six weeks for delivery. For purchase over $10.00 you may use VISA: card number, expiration date and customer signature must be included.

Name _____

Address _____

City _____ State/Zip _____

VISA Card # _____ Exp.Date _____

Signature _____ 1146-14

Is The Roller Coaster Really Haunted?

THE BEAST

❑ 88055-1/$3.99

It Was An Awsome Ride—Through Time!

THE BEAST 2

❑ 52951-X/$3.99

 A MINSTREL® BOOK

Published by Pocket Books